Robin Hill School

Fall Leaf Project!

Written by Margaret McNamara
Illustrated by Mike Gordon

Ready-to-Read
Aladdin
New York   London   Toronto   Sydney

For Barbara Bowen, a born teacher

❦

ALADDIN PAPERBACKS
An imprint of Simon & Schuster Children's Publishing Division
1230 Avenue of the Americas, New York, NY 10020
Text copyright © 2006 by Brenda Bowen
Illustrations copyright © 2006 by Mike Gordon
All rights reserved, including the right of reproduction in whole or in part in any form.
READY-TO-READ is a registered trademark of Simon & Schuster, Inc.
ALADDIN PAPERBACKS and colophon are trademarks of Simon & Schuster, Inc.
Designed by Sammy Yuen Jr.
The text of this book was set in CentSchbook.
Manufactured in the United States of America
First Aladdin edition October 2006
8 10 9
0614 LAK

Library of Congress Cataloging-in-Publication Data
McNamara, Margaret.
Fall leaf project / by Margaret McNamara ;
illustrated by Mike Gordon.— 1st Aladdin Paperbacks ed.
p. cm. — (Robin Hill School) (Ready-to-read)
Summary: Mrs. Connor's first-grade class decides to send colorful
fall leaves to students in another state where the leaves do not change color.
ISBN-13: 978-1-4169-1537-9 (pbk.)
ISBN-10: 1-4169-1537-0 (pbk.)
ISBN-13: 978-1-4169-1538-6 (library binding)
ISBN-10: 1-4169-1538-9 (library binding)
[1. Autumn—Fiction. 2. Leaves—Fiction. 3. Schools—Fiction.]
I. Gordon, Mike, ill. II. Title. III. Series.
PZ7.M232518Fal 2006   [E]—dc22   2005030951

Mrs. Connor's class
was learning about fall.
Mrs. Connor showed
the class a map.

"In our state," she said,
"leaves change color.

In other states,
they do not."

"Oh, no!" said Emma.

"We have so many
fall leaves,"
said Hannah.
"Can we share them?"

"Good idea,"
said Mrs. Connor.
"I know a teacher
in a state where the leaves
do not change.

His name is Mr. Soto.
We can send leaves
to his class."

Mrs. Connor's class
went outside.

"Gather your favorite leaves," said Mrs. Connor.

Kate chose seven
yellow leaves.

Ayanna chose nine
orange leaves.

Jamie liked red leaves
the best.
He chose eleven of them.

"Watch me!" said Charles.
Charles jumped into
a great big pile
of leaves.

Becky, Emma, and Hannah
sorted the leaves
they found.
"Oak, oak, oak,"
said Hannah.

"Maple, maple," said Becky.

"Chestnut," said Emma.

"What is this one?"
asked Hannah.
It looked like a mitten.
"That is sassafras!"
said Mrs. Connor.

Back in the classroom,
the first-graders
got to work.
Nia wrote.

Reza glued.

Eigen wrapped.

Mrs. Connor packed.

Hannah licked the stamps.

"There," said Mrs. Connor.
"Our project is done."

Three days later
Mr. Soto's first-graders
opened the package.

They decorated
their classroom
with the leaves.

They sent a letter
to Mrs. Connor's class.

Dear First-Graders
of Robin Hill School,
Thank you for the leaves.

We love the colors.
We love the shapes.
Your friends,
Mr. Soto's First-Graders

P.S. Happy fall!